JOURNEY TO THE CENTRE OF THE EARTH

Based on the novel by Jules Verne
Adapted by Sarah Courtauld
Illustrated by Andrea Da Rold

Reading consultant: Alison Kelly
University of Roehampton

Contents

Chapter 1

A Mystery to be Solved

It was a peaceful spring morning when my uncle, Professor Liedenbrock, came bursting into our house. He strode through the dining room where I sat, shouted, "Axel, follow me!" and stormed into his study.

I hadn't had time to move before he yelled, "We-ell? Where are you? Aren't you here yet?"

My uncle was not a bad man but he was certainly an eccentric. He had a clear, scientific mind – and a terrifying temper. Every stride he took was exactly three feet long, and, while he walked, he waved his arms about. With such a man, the only thing to do was obey him, so I hurried to his study.

I found him buried in his armchair,
holding a tattered, ancient-looking book.

"Axel, come, look at this priceless gem.
It's an ancient chronicle from Iceland..."

"How, er, magnificent," I said, not very
convincingly. What was the point of making
a fuss over a dusty old book?

As my uncle started talking about ancient
runes, my mind drifted off to thoughts of
Grauben, my sweetheart.

I was lost in a dream, thinking about how beautiful she was, while my uncle nattered on... until a piece of parchment fell out of the book and slipped to the floor.

"But what's this?" said my uncle, picking it up. He carefully spread the parchment out across his desk, and we stared at the strange characters written across it.

As we were studying the parchment, Martha, my uncle's maid, put her head around the door.

"Soup is served," she said meekly.

"The devil take your soup!" shouted my uncle. "I'm not going to eat or sleep until I can read this parchment."

I stood up to go to lunch.

"And nor will you Axel!" he roared.

Martha fled.

Two hours later, my uncle had translated

the ancient runes into our language, but it still didn't make any sense.

"It must be in code," he said. "Possibly written by someone who owned the book."

Picking up his magnifying glass, he scanned the book, until he came across a faded name: Arne Saknussemm.

"Arne Saknussemm," he muttered. "A brilliant explorer of the sixteenth century. Could he have written this? But in what code... Axel!" he said abruptly. "What do you think?"

I shrugged. It seemed likely to me that the message meant nothing at all.

"It just doesn't make any sense!" my uncle growled, slamming the desk with his fist. Then, darting across the study and hurtling downstairs like an avalanche, he rushed out onto the street and raced off.

CHAPTER 2

A TERRIFYING SECRET

That afternoon, sitting in my uncle's study, I couldn't help trying to solve the puzzle. It whirled around my head, until the letters began to dance in the air, and I felt as if I would suffocate.

"I give up," I cried, fanning myself with the translation.

Looking up, I caught sight of the back. The letters were still visible through the paper, and reading them backwards... they suddenly made sense. My mind sparked.

I'd found the truth by accident. You can imagine how excited I felt. Then I read the whole message – and was petrified. It described a journey. A terrifying journey.

"No!" I thought. "I can't tell my uncle about this. He'd demand that we go and we'd never come back!"

I picked up the paper, and was about to throw it into the fire, when the door opened, and my uncle strode in.

He spent the rest of the day at his desk, staring at the parchment and his translation.

The next morning, he was still there, with red, bleary eyes. I felt sorry for him, but I couldn't tell him the solution. I didn't want to be responsible for his death.

That morning, when I tried to leave the house, I realized that my uncle had locked us all in. By lunchtime, I was ravenous – and there was nothing to eat in the house.

Two o'clock chimed. The situation was becoming ridiculous. We were *starving*. I told myself that I had exaggerated the importance of the document. Perhaps I could tell my uncle the message after all. In any case, would he really believe what it said?

"Uncle?" I said hesitantly. "Look. It makes sense. Not read from the front, but if you hold the paper up to the light and read through the back..."

"So simple!" roared my uncle. "Clever old Saknussemm wrote it back-to-front!"

Grabbing the parchment, he read:

Go down into the crater of Snaefells Yocul, O audacious voyager, and you will reach the middle of the Earth.
I did it. Arne Saknussemm

My uncle jumped up as if he had been electrified. He paced around and threw punches. At last, he calmed down and flung himself into his armchair.

"Pack my trunk. And yours too."

"Uncle, I-"

"Now!"

"Surely it's a joke?" I insisted.

"If it is, we'll find out soon enough."

"But where is this 'Snaefells Yocul'? And what does the message mean?"

"That's easy. Snaefell is in Iceland. It's an extinct volcano. And its crater leads directly to the centre of the Earth!"

"But that's impossible!"

"Says who?"

"Well, the scientific theories..."

"Oh, the theories! Some daft theories! They're not going to stop us, those silly little theories..."

"But uncle, according to science, the Earth is full of molten fire!"

"Well?" my uncle thundered. "Are you

afraid of melting! Stop hanging around like a drip. We leave tomorrow morning!"

I knew I couldn't change his mind, but the idea of climbing down into the Earth filled me with pure terror. I thought at least Grauben would agree that the plan was crazy, and persuade my uncle to give up the whole idea. But, to my horror, Grauben was thrilled by our expedition.

That night, I had a series of terrible nightmares. I was trapped underground, plunging through endless darkness.

In the morning, pale and trembling, I said goodbye to Grauben, and we set sail. Only a few weeks later, our ship docked in Iceland.

Within a day, my uncle had found a guide, Hans, to lead us up Mount Snaefells. Hans was a calm and silent man, who spoke not one word of our language. All too soon, we were standing at the base of the volcano, gazing up at its snowy peak.

CHAPTER 3

INTO THE EARTH

We walked up the volcano in single file, battered by an icy wind, Hans striding ahead. Every time I stopped to catch my breath, he turned around and slowly shook his head at me, and I was forced to struggle on.

When I looked back over my shoulder, I saw why he wouldn't let me rest. Behind us, a column of freezing mist was rising steadily. We had to hurry up the mountain to stay ahead of it.

That night, we slept on the peak. The next morning, we woke stiff and half-frozen, and began to climb down into the craggy crater itself.

The descent was hard work, but my spirits lifted as we went. I was sure the crater would just come to a dead end, and that soon we'd be climbing back out and heading home.

But at the bottom of the crater were three vast chimneys, through which the volcano had once erupted. And, on one, we saw two carved initials: A.S.

"Arne Saknussemm!" my uncle grinned. "Can you have any doubt now? Here it is! The chimney that leads to the middle of the Earth!"

I looked down into the darkness, faint with fear.

"Forward!" my uncle declared, his eyes shining with excitement.

If it had been just my uncle, perhaps I could have refused. But with Hans there, so composed, I felt too ashamed to admit my terror. My uncle rigged up a rope, shared out the tools and provisions, and one by one we headed into the blackness.

After over three hours of climbing down the narrow shaft, we reached the bottom – and there, in front of us, was a passageway.

"Off we go," my uncle said cheerfully, switching on our lanterns.

Looking up, I could see one beautiful, blue circle of sky, far above me. With a knot of fear in my stomach, and trembling hands, I followed him.

For days, we stumbled through twisting, turning tunnels. Sometimes the walls were

covered in a thick, glistening coat of slime.
At other times they glittered, as if we were
inside an enormous diamond.

There was a deadly quietness under the
Earth. We walked in silence through vast
caverns, and crawled on our bellies through
narrow, hot tunnels, with the walls pressing
in on all sides. We held our breath as we
groped through passages that stank of
rotten eggs, and gasped as we came out into
caves as big as cathedrals, with hundreds of
stalactites hanging above us.

Each day took us deeper. There was only one problem. My uncle had been sure that we would find water in underground springs, and so far we had found none.

My uncle was in such a terrible temper that I didn't dare mention it until we were in grave danger. "Uncle," I said finally, "we only have one more day's supply of water."

"And?"

"What if we run out?"

He turned on me, glaring. "So, you have run out of courage too?" he asked.

I didn't know what to say. I had long wondered if he was crazy – now I knew.

We rationed what remained of the water, but soon there was only a trickle left. I felt dizzy with thirst but carried on, until, nearly passing out, I fell to my knees.

"Uncle, we have to go back," I begged.

"Now?" my uncle said. "When our expedition has the greatest chance of success? You go back and take Hans."

"What, and leave you here?" I asked.

"Yes, leave me here," he said. "I started this expedition, and I will carry it out to the end. I will not return."

I was so dismayed, I couldn't answer.

"I am sure there are springs in the rock," he went on. "Why not give me one more day? If we don't find water tomorrow, we will all turn back."

I feared that tomorrow would be too late. We would be too far from the surface of the Earth. I realized, dimly, that I would never see my home, or Grauben, again. But I got to my feet and staggered after him.

The next day, we were still shuffling along. I was now so dizzy, I hardly knew where I was.

"The springs must be close now," my uncle muttered.

At that moment, I felt my legs give way. My uncle bent over me.

"It's over," he said, as my eyes closed.

I don't know how much time passed, but when I opened my eyes again, I saw my uncle rolled up in his blanket, and I remembered his words. *It's over.* I knew I was too weak to get back to the surface of the Earth. I would die here. We would all die, here, together.

Hearing a noise, I turned my head to see Hans slip away down the tunnel holding the lamp. Where was he going? Was he abandoning us?

A few hours later, I was woken by feet stomping up the passageway. Hans shook my uncle. "Vatten," he said.

"You've found water?" said my uncle.

Hans pointed downwards. A minute before, I couldn't move. But at the thought of water, I got to my feet. It didn't take us long to pack up and start walking again.

Soon we could hear a stream, rumbling along, on the other side of a rock.

Hans swung his pickaxe, striking the wall of the tunnel again and again. After an hour, there was a whistling noise, and a jet of water spurted out of the rock.

I yelped as I touched it – the water was
boiling hot. But soon it was flowing along
the ground, cooling down, and we gulped
our first delicious mouthfuls. Where did it
come from? I didn't care.

"Tastes like ink," said my uncle, happily.

After drinking it, we all fell into a deep
and peaceful sleep.

CHAPTER 4

LOST

The next day I felt like a new man, determined to go a long way. We marched along twisting granite corridors, the stream of water following at our feet.

By August 7th, according to my uncle's calculations, we had reached a depth of 90 miles. I remember that day, because I was walking ahead. My uncle was carrying one lamp, and I carried the other, and when I looked around for a moment, I realized that both he and Hans had gone.

At first, I wasn't worried. I thought I had been walking too fast, so I simply walked back up the tunnel. It stayed empty.

"Hello? Hello! HELLO!"

There was no reply. A shudder ran

through me. "Be calm," I told myself. I walked back for another hour. Still, there was no one there.

I told myself that I wasn't lost, only bewildered. After all, there was only one tunnel. Besides, I had a clue – the stream running at my feet would guide me back to my uncle. I bent down to wash my face in it, and found that it was no longer there.

It is impossible to describe how I felt then. Somehow, I had taken a side turning and now I was lost, miles under the Earth. How could I find my uncle again? All around me was absolute silence.

I felt as if all the rock above me was weighing down on my shoulders and crushing me. Which way should I go? Up. I started striding up the tunnel, as fast as I could. I marched for hours, until I hit a solid wall of rock. My last hope was shattered. My lamp fell to the floor, spluttered and went out.

As the darkness closed in on me, I lost my

head. I stood up and started to stagger, then run back along the passage in the pitch black. I yelled as I ran, bruising myself on the rock – but I just kept running.

After what felt like hours, I tripped again, and this time crashed into a wall of cold, hard rock. I collapsed to the floor and my eyes closed.

When I next opened my eyes, my face was hot and wet, covered in tears and blood. I thought that I could hear voices, but it was just my imagination.

I heard the noises again. It must be an echo of my own voice, I thought – I must have been crying out. Then I really did hear someone speaking and called out, "Uncle? Uncle Liedenbrock!"

"Axel? Is it you?" My uncle's voice was faint and far away. "My boy, where are you?"

"Lost in deepest darkness!"

"Where is your lamp?"

"Out!"

"And the stream?"

"Disappeared!"

"Axel, take courage. Listen to me. Start walking down the passage, and we will walk towards you."

I dragged myself up, and started limping down the passageway, as fast as I could. The tunnel soon became steeper, and then the ground fell away and there was nothing but air beneath me. My head struck a rock and I knew no more.

Chapter 5

The sea

When I next woke, I was lying in a small cave. Beyond its mouth, I could see the light of day, and hear the wind blowing and waves breaking on a beach. My uncle came over to me.

"Am I dreaming?"

"Not at all."

"I'm crazy then. I can see sunlight."

"Don't worry, my boy. All will soon become clear. We found you, and brought you here. You've been resting. Tomorrow we shall sail," he added, as if it was the most normal thing in the world.

"Sail?" The word was too much for my curiosity. I managed to drag myself to the mouth of the cave, and stopped still.

"The SEA!" I shouted. I could actually see the sea. But how could there be a *sea* under the Earth?

We were inside what must have been a cavern, but it was far too vast to call it that. The sea stretched into the distance, trees lining the shore. Above my head, clouds swept across a sky. Above them, there must have been rock, but the cavern was several miles high.

"Hans has been making a raft," my uncle said calmly, "and tomorrow we shall set out. According to my calculations, the sea is 70 miles across – the journey should take four days."

I could hardly believe it, but the next day, we set sail, my uncle humming with excitement.

The humming didn't last and nor did the excitement. After a week, we still hadn't reached the other side. My uncle's patience was wearing thin.

"I didn't come this far to go on a silly boat trip," he growled.

Soon, we had more to worry about. We lowered an icepick over the raft, to try to find out how deep the sea was, and it came back covered in bite marks.

"Teeth," my uncle said. "And why not?"

I stared at him. Surely there couldn't be anything *alive* in this sea? The next few days were quiet. Each night I dreamed of terrifying, gigantic creatures, gliding below us. But I dismissed my fears as ridiculous... until our raft was hit by an enormous jolt.

"What was that?" my uncle shouted. "Have we hit the coast?"

Hans pointed to vast objects in the water.

"A giant porpoise!" I cried.

"And a sea serpent," my uncle added.

"Look, a whale!" I shouted, "And a monstrous crocodile!"

I stared in horror at these enormous creatures – just one of them could crush the raft with a single bite. Hans tried to steer our little raft away, but they swam closer, faster than express trains.

I held up my rifle to shoot – but what effect could a tiny bullet have on one of these monsters?

As we watched, the creatures reared up out of the water, and we realized there were just two: a monster with a porpoise's snout and crocodile's teeth, and an enormous sea lizard.

They were dinosaurs!

"An Icthyosaurus and a Plesiosaurus," my uncle murmured. "Still alive, down here. Incredible!"

There was an eerie silence as the monsters paused, facing each other. Then, ignoring our raft, each attacked the other with incredible fury. They hissed and thrashed in the water. Each slap of a tail, and each claw tearing through the ocean sent liquid mountains racing towards us. We nearly toppled off the raft.

They fought for two hours before they both disappeared beneath the surface, leaving a whirlpool behind.

For a moment all was still. Then the head of the Plesiosaurus reared back up, covered in blood. I could see it was mortally wounded.

It thrashed the water like a gigantic whip, and the spray nearly blinded us. After some time, it slowed down. Finally, it was still, and its lifeless body floated away on the waves.

Chapter 6

The Storm

The clouds were dark; the sea was calm. The sky felt heavy with electricity. My hair stood on end. You could almost smell the storm coming.

"Seems as if we might be in for some bad weather," I said.

My uncle didn't reply, and scowled as he looked out to sea. It was three weeks since we'd set sail. There was no land in sight.

"Let's take down the sail and lower the mast in case we're hit by lightning."

"No, a hundred times no!" my uncle declared. "If there's a storm, it can take us on. I don't care if the raft is smashed to smithereens, as long as we get to the far shore."

As he spoke, the storm hit us. The sail stretched out like a bubble about to burst, and the raft started to hurtle across the sea at an incredible speed.

"The sail! We need to take down the sail!" I shouted.

"No!" my uncle yelled back – and we raced across the sea like madmen.

Streaks of lightning crashed down
around us, thunder clapped overhead and
hailstones pelted onto the deck.

The sea seemed as if it was alight. Each
wave was a fire-breathing beast. I held as
tight as I could to the mast, which bent like
a reed in the storm. All that night, and all
the following day, the boat raced onwards.
On the second day of the storm,
there was a terrible cracking sound,
and the sail was carried off by the
wind, flying high into the sky.

The next moment, a ball of fire appeared on the edge of the raft. It was half white, half electric blue, and it rolled up to me, landing about an inch away from my feet. Everything on the deck became white hot. The ball burst – all I could see was flames – then everything went out.

CHAPTER 7

THE SHORE AT LAST

I don't remember clearly what happened next. Somehow, the battered raft reached the shore. The next morning, I was lying, feeling half-dead, on a beach.

Hans was his usual, silent self, but my uncle was in a worryingly cheerful mood. "Sleep soundly?" he asked.

"Oh – perfectly," I said. "Every bone in my body aches. But I expect I'll be alright."

"Of course you will," he replied.

"You seem very happy this morning," I said cautiously.

"Delighted, my boy, delighted! Now we have crossed the sea, and we can plunge further into the depths of the Earth."

Hearing that, I knew my uncle was even

crazier than I thought. "Uncle, can I ask you a question?"

"Certainly, Axel."

"How are we going to get home?"

"Either we will find a new route, or we will come right back along the same path. I don't imagine the route will disappear behind us." He smiled.

He made it all sound so simple.

After a quick meal, we decided to work out how far we had come. But when my uncle got out his compass, the arrow pointed the wrong way. We stared at each other. There was only one conclusion.

Somehow, in the storm, the boat had turned around – and we had come right back to the shore that we'd started from.

"Impossible!" he said.

"Maybe we were never supposed to cross the sea," I said excitedly. "We thought we were following Saknussemm's route...

but who knows if he crossed the sea..."

"No," my uncle replied. "We must set out again. Hans will simply rebuild the raft. While he does, we shall explore."

So my uncle and I set out to explore the shore. Before long, we stumbled across an eerie sight – a field full of bones. We trampled over fossils and rattling, ancient skeletons, while white mounds of bones rose in the distance.

There were more dinosaur skeletons in that field than in all the museums in the world. But something more astonishing was to come.

"Look, Axel..."

I followed my uncle's gaze, and was struck dumb. Before us was the crumbling mummy of what had once been a primitive man. Its black, hollow eyes stared at us.

After some moments of silence, my uncle was himself again. "Come on," he said. "There must be more to explore."

Beyond the field was a thick forest, full of towering trees. My uncle stepped briskly into the cool shadows. Reluctantly, I followed him. All sorts of strange creatures must once have lived down here. Could they live here still?

For an hour we walked in silence, before I stopped, and grabbed my uncle's arm. I thought I saw – no, I really did see – enormous animals wandering under the trees. I heard their ivory tusks as they tore bark from the trees. Branches cracked as great clumps of leaves disappeared into their huge mouths.

"Come on! Forward!" my uncle whispered.

"No!" I hissed to him. We were unarmed. "No human creature can hope to survive those beasts..."

"No human creature?" my uncle interrupted. "Look over there. I can see a creature who looks almost human!"

I looked, shrugging my shoulders, determined not to believe him. But there, beneath a towering tree, was a giant of a man – more than twelve feet tall.

We stood still for a moment, completely speechless. I panicked that he'd spot us.

"Run for it!" I shouted, dragging my uncle behind me, and we ran like mad until we reached the edge of the forest.

Now, when I consider it calmly, I cannot believe what we saw. Our eyes must have been mistaken. No race of men could possibly live in that underground world.

We were on our way back to Hans, when I spotted a dagger. "We must have dropped this earlier," I muttered.

"So you brought this with you?" my uncle asked, frowning.

I looked at the knife more closely. "No... Didn't you?"

"No," said my uncle. "And nor did Hans. It's most peculiar."

He turned over the rusty knife in his

hands. "This is from the sixteenth century."

"Do you mean..."

"This blade has been lying here for the past two hundred years. It belonged to a man who used a knife to engrave his name on the rocks."

"Arne Saknussemm!"

"Yes – he must have used it to mark his name once more on the route to the centre. Let's find it."

We worked our way along the high cliffs, looking for anything that might turn into a passageway. Eventually, we came to two rocks. Between them was a dark tunnel and there, on a slab of granite, two letters were carved, half eaten away by time:

A S

It was Arne Saknussemm once again.

When I saw those letters, all my fears dissolved and I was ready to rush headlong into the tunnel.

"Stop! We must get Hans," said my uncle.

"Fine. But then we can go straight down."

"Yes. We're getting there."

We collected Hans, and soon all three of us were marching through the tunnel, but after only about twenty feet, we stopped.

"Bother!" said my uncle. Rocks blocked the only way forward. There was no way around them.

"They must have fallen down since Saknussemm's journey," my uncle said. "If we can't beat them, we don't deserve to get to the centre of the Earth." He glowered at the rocks. "We could get through with pickaxes," he said, at last.

"It's too hard for the pickaxes."

"An icepick then."

"It's too deep for an icepick."

"Well then, gunpowder, an explosion! Let's mine the obstacle and blow it up."

"Blow it up?"

"Why not? It's only a bit of rock! Hans, to work!" shouted my uncle.

So Hans began, hollowing out a cavity for the explosive.

It was not an easy task. He had to make a hole big enough to fit a large amount of gunpowder. While Hans worked, I helped my uncle to make the fuse. At midnight, our work was complete. All we needed was a spark to set it off...

CHAPTER 8

BLAST

Every time I think about the next day, terror makes my heart beat faster. From that moment on, our reason, our own actions had no influence on events. We became the playthings of the Earth.

We were up by six in the morning. The plan was to take the raft out to sea, to reduce the danger to us from the explosion. According to our calculations, the fuse would burn for ten minutes before setting off the powder. I asked permission to light the fuse.

"Ready?" my uncle yelled, from the edge of the shore.

"Ready."

"Fire away, my lad!" my uncle shouted.

I lit the fuse, and it spluttered into life as I sprinted from the tunnel to the beach. With a hard shove, Hans pushed us off, and the raft drifted out across the waves.

"Five minutes more... Four... Three..." the Professor counted out.

My heart beat every half-second.

"Two... One... Take that, granite mountains!"

What happened next? The shapes of the rocks actually changed before my eyes: they swung away like curtains.

I glimpsed a huge hole, hollowed out in the shore. The sea became one immense wave, the raft shot up like an arrow and the three of us were thrown off our feet.

In a second, everything was plunged into darkness. I felt the raft bucking beneath me and clung on tight. I tried to speak to my uncle, but with the waters crashing around me I couldn't hear a thing.

Despite the darkness, the noise, the terror and the surprise, I soon understood what must have happened.

Behind the blocked passageway, there was an enormous hole. The explosion had set off an earthquake, the Earth had opened up, and the sea, which was now more like a river, was sweeping us into it.

One hour, two hours went by. We had been in utter darkness, so I was quite surprised to see a light beside me. Hans' calm face appeared, as he shone a flickering light into the blackness.

We were on a vast, swirling river, steeper than any rapids I could imagine. The raft swept on, and my uncle and I looked at each other with wild, staring eyes.

Hours passed, as the water carried us

deeper and deeper into the Earth. I realized with a start that nearly all of our food had been swept away.

But why was I worrying about food? We'd never get back from these depths. We'd die down here, either dashed against the rocks, or drowned, or eaten by sea monsters...

Still, I held a tiny flicker of hope in my heart. I did not know how we could escape the furious river. I didn't know how I could ever see Grauben again. But there was always a chance. Maybe only a chance in a thousand, but that is still a chance.

I thought of trying to tell my uncle that our food was nearly all gone, but I stayed silent. Hans' lantern dimmed, and then went out, and I closed my eyes to shut out the darkness.

After a while, our speed grew even faster. Now, we seemed to be falling. We gripped each other's arms so tightly, we left bruises. After some time – I don't know how long – the raft abruptly stopped falling. Colossal waves crashed down over us.

We were drowning!

After a few seconds, I gulped air again.

The roaring of the water stopped.

"We're going up!" my uncle murmured.

"What do you mean?"

"We're climbing! We're actually climbing!"

I stretched out my arms. I touched the wall and cut my hand as it scraped on the rock, we were rising so fast.

"A lamp! A lamp!" my uncle shouted.

Hans managed to light one.

"Exactly as I thought," my uncle said. "We have reached a narrow shaft. The water is rising up it, and taking us with it."

"Where to?"

"I don't know. But we'll have to be ready for anything. At this rate, we'll get to the top in no time."

"Yes – if the shaft has a way out. If the top is blocked, we'll be crushed to death!"

CHAPTER 9

CRUSHED

"Axel," my uncle said, "we may die at any moment. But we may also be saved. We should be ready to seize any advantage. Let's eat to build our strength."

"Ah..." I said. "I'm sorry, uncle, but-"

"What? Has something happened?"

"This is all we have left," I said. "A few biscuits... and one piece of dried meat for the three of us."

My uncle looked at me blankly, as if he couldn't understand.

"Well," I said, "do you still think we might be saved?"

He did not reply.

An hour passed. I was desperately hungry, so was Hans, and so was my uncle.

No one dared eat the pathetic remains of the food. We were still climbing fast. The temperature was rising fast, too. Sweat poured off my face, and my clothes were soaked through.

"We must eat the last of the food," my uncle said, finally. "Alright, this meal will be our last. But at least, instead of being exhausted, we will be men again!"

My uncle took the piece of meat and the few biscuits, divided them into three and handed them out, and we ate in silence.

We had eaten our last meal. It was five in the morning. Afterwards, we were all lost in our thoughts.

"We're climbing, still climbing," my uncle said. "But where? Who knows..."

He had been looking closely at the walls of the shaft for an hour. Meanwhile, it was still getting hotter. We had all taken off our jackets and waistcoats. The heat was almost too much to bear.

When I looked at the compass, it had

gone crazy. The needle swung wildly.

"Uncle, we've had it!"

"I think, my boy," my uncle replied, "you are mistaken. I'm hoping for something to save us... an eruption."

"An eruption?"

"I believe we are in the vent of a volcano. It's the best thing that could have happened to us."

"What? Being in the middle of an eruption with lava and boiling water beneath us, about to be spat out into the air in a whirlwind of flame, with rock and showers of ash – and that's the best thing that could have happened to us?"

"Yes," said my uncle. "For it's the only chance we have of returning to the surface of the Earth."

My uncle was right. He had never seemed more fearless. The noise and the heat became greater and greater.

Wild, glowing lights shone in the walls of the chimney. As we rushed upwards, flames licked and crackled on the walls.

"Sulphur flames!" I shouted.

"Oh yes," my uncle said calmly. "Nothing could be more normal during an eruption."

Underneath us, the raft was floating on a stream of lava. The heat was unbearable. Gradually my mind stopped working altogether. I have no clear memory of what happened during the next few hours.

I remember endless blasts of heat. Our raft rose and fell on waves of lava. My last thought was of a circus performer fastened to the mouth of a cannon, at the moment when the shot goes off and sends him flying into the air.

CHAPTER 10

ALL'S WELL THAT ENDS WELL

When I next opened my eyes, I felt the strong hand of our guide clutching my belt. With the other he was holding my uncle. I was shaken, bruised and aching all over. Blinding sunlight burned my eyes. I blinked, and saw that I was lying on a mountain side, a few feet from the edge of a cliff. Hans had saved my life while I lay on the edge of the crater.

"Where are we?" said my uncle, looking slightly annoyed to be back on Earth again.

Hans shrugged his shoulders.

"It doesn't look much like Iceland," my uncle continued.

I looked around. Above us, the crater was sending flame and ashes into the air.

Far below us were green meadows. I could see an olive grove, and beyond it, the smooth blue sea.

"Let's get out of here," said my uncle, "before we're crushed by falling rocks."

I felt as if I could hardly move. Still, we struggled down the steep slopes of the volcano, and after two hours marching, we reached the countryside.

There, between some rocks, was a spring. We plunged our hands and faces into the fresh water, then plucked pomegranates from nearby trees, sucking on the cool, sweet fruit. The juice dribbled down my chin, and I lay back on the sweet-smelling grass, and felt the sun against my eyelids. It felt good to be back on top of the Earth.

While we were lying under the trees, a ragged looking child appeared. Just as he was about to dart away, Hans grabbed him.

"What island is this?" asked my uncle.

The boy stared at him blankly.

My uncle, who was proud of knowing

many languages, tried his best French. "Quelle est cette île, mon enfant?"

Silence.

"Maybe Italian..." said my uncle. "Come si chiama questa isola?"

"Stromboli," said the little boy, slipping out of Hans' grip and racing away.

"Stromboli!" I murmured.

So we were in Italy, in the middle of the Mediterranean, and the terrible volcano was Stromboli. We had entered the Earth by one volcano, and ended up being thrown out of another, nearly 3,000 miles away.

That was the end of our journey.

After another delightful meal of fruit and cold water, we set out for the port. It would not have been wise to tell anyone how we had ended up there, so we pretended to be shipwrecked sailors, and soon we were on a boat, bound for home.

I will not even attempt to describe how happy I was to return to Hamburg, and to Grauben, my sweetheart.

At first, few people believed our story, but gradually, they began to change their minds. My uncle, a persuasive man, became famous, and the book of our adventure created a sensation all over the world. My uncle went on many more travels. I did not.

"Now you are a hero, Axel," Grauben said, "you need never go away again."

I promised that I wouldn't and I have been more than happy to keep my word.

Jules Verne (1828-1905)

Jules Verne was a French author who became famous for his extravagant, fantastical adventure stories. He wrote about air, space and underwater travel before air travel, practical submarines and spaceships were invented.

There is a story that, when he was twelve, he sneaked onto a ship bound for India, and was found and whipped by his father.

"From now on, I shall travel only in my imagination," he is reported to have said.

His most famous novels include *Twenty Thousand Leagues Under The Sea* and *Around The World In Eighty Days*.

Designed by Samantha Barrett
Series designer: Russell Punter
Series editor: Lesley Sims

First published in 2013 by Usborne Publishing Ltd., Usborne House,
83-85 Saffron Hill, London EC1N 8RT, England. www.usborne.com
Copyright © 2013 Usborne Publishing Ltd.